Football Fiasco!

By **Elizabeth Dale**

Illustrated by
Ramona Bruno

Kaz was so excited. Her football team, Chimps United, was playing Treetop Swingers in the Jungle Cup. She was a sub, so she wasn't in the team yet, but she was there ready to join if any player couldn't play. And their manager, Janetta, was smiling at her.

**The item should be returned or renewed
by the last date stamped below.**

Dylid dychwelyd neu adnewyddu'r eitem erbyn
y dyddiad olaf sydd wedi'i stampio isod.

20-03-24.

To renew visit / Adnewyddwch ar
www.newport.gov.uk/libraries

Early Readers

'Football Fiasco!'
An original concept by Elizabeth Dale
© Elizabeth Dale 2023

Illustrated by Ramona Bruno

Published by MAVERICK ARTS PUBLISHING LTD
Studio 11, City Business Centre, 6 Brighton Road,
Horsham, West Sussex, RH13 5BB
© Maverick Arts Publishing Limited May 2023
+44 (0)1403 256941

A CIP catalogue record for this book is available at the British Library.

ISBN 978-1-84886-957-8

www.maverickbooks.co.uk

This book is rated as: Turquoise Band (Guided Reading)

"Our central defender, Suzy, has left the team," said Janetta. "Will you be the central defender, Kaz?"

Kaz frowned. She longed to play in attack, not defence...

Mia, Kaz's friend, said, "I'd love to be a defender. Can Kaz take my place as striker and I'll be a defender?"

"If that's okay with you, Kaz?" asked Janetta.

"Yes!" grinned Kaz. "Thanks, Mia!"

As soon as the game started, Kaz waited to be passed the ball... and waited... and waited.

But Chimps United's defenders just couldn't get the ball away from their own goal.
Kaz realised that if she was going to show everyone how good she was, she'd have to go and collect the ball herself!

Kaz raced back to her own team's goal, just as the ball soared across it. She jumped high, higher than every other player, and managed to head the ball. Brilliant!

"Goal!"

No! Kaz couldn't believe it. She had headed the ball into her own goal! As the Treetop Swingers celebrated, Kaz's team-mates stared at her in horror.

"I'm so sorry!" she whispered, fighting back tears. "I'll make it up to you, I promise."

Kaz was so upset at her
terrible mistake,
she just couldn't
focus on the game.
She missed easy
passes to her and
mis-kicked the ball.

She even kicked
it straight to a
Treetop player
who had a clear
shot at the goal.

Fortunately, Jo, United's goalie, saved the
goal. But Janetta called Kaz off the pitch
and put Asha on instead. Kaz felt awful.
She'd totally messed up her chance to show
how good she was. What a fiasco!

"I'm so sorry," she told Janetta. "I've played terribly."

"You just need to calm down," said Janetta, hugging her.

Kaz stood miserably on the touchline, willing her team to score. But Treetop blocked every shot.

At half-time, Jo limped off the pitch.

"I think I've sprained my ankle," she said.

"Oh dear," said Janetta, "you can't play on."

"That's okay," said Jo. "I get really nervous playing goalie anyway."

"Kaz, you're our last sub," said Janetta. "Will you be our goalie?"

Kaz gulped, then smiled bravely. She'd never been goalie before. But she owed it to the team to try – and not let in too many goals!

"Here, wear this. Don't look so worried," said Janetta. "Whilst we'd love to win, it's more important to have fun!"

Treetop attacked the moment the second half started. As the first shot cannoned towards her, Kaz forgot her fears. She dived and pushed the ball away. Hooray!

United's supporters cheered loudly and Kaz smiled. Maybe she could do this?

But Treetop had a corner. They sent the ball
high towards the goal...

Kaz jumped above everyone and caught it.

Everybody cheered again. This was fun!

Kaz kicked the ball well into the other half

towards Asha. Asha ran and shot...

"Goal!"

Hooray! United had equalised!

"That's thanks to you, Kaz," Mia yelled.

"That was a brilliant pass."

Kaz was thrilled. So she could help score

goals, even as a goalie! Hopefully she'd made

up for her mistake.

Treetop quickly attacked, but Kaz managed to save every shot. And when she threw the ball to Asha far into Treetop's half, Asha scored again.

United were in the lead – with minutes to go!

They could win – Kaz was sure of it!

But Treetop started attacking even harder.

As Mia desperately tried to block a shot,

the ball struck her arm. The whistle blew.

"Penalty!" the ref called.

No! Mia was horrified, but not as much as Kaz, who'd never tried to save a penalty before! "Don't worry, Kaz, you can do it!" said Asha. Kaz smiled nervously.

The Treetop striker ran forward and – WHAM! She struck the ball hard towards the top corner of the goal.

Kaz leapt as high as she could – and caught it!

United and their supporters cheered.

Then the ref blew her whistle.

"No! What's wrong?!" Kaz cried.

"Nothing!" yelled Mia. "That signals

the end of the game. We've won!"

"And all thanks to you, Kaz," said Janetta.

"You won the match for us!"

"Go, Kaz! Go, Kaz!" everyone chanted in

agreement.

"Can Kaz always be our goalie now?" Jo asked

Janetta. "She's far better than me and I'd

rather play in defence."

"That would be great if you'd like that,

Kaz?" said Janetta. "Being a goalie is just as

important as any other position in the team."

Kaz smiled. It *was* important, she realised that now. And she was a far better goalie than striker! "I'd absolutely love to be goalie!" she said, and as everyone cheered, she swung along the crossbar in celebration!

10

Quiz

1. What is the name of Kaz's team?
a) Chimps United
b) Treetop Swingers
c) Jungle Climbers

2. What happens after Kaz heads the ball?
a) She gets a penalty
b) She misses the goal
c) She scores an own goal

3. Who hurts their ankle?
a) Asha
b) Jo
c) Kaz

4. Who takes Jo's place as goalie?

a) Kaz

b) Mia

c) Janetta

5. How does Kaz celebrate at the end of the match?

a) She runs around the pitch

b) She does a dance

c) She swings along the crossbar

Turn over for answers

Book Bands for Guided Reading

The Institute of Education book banding system is a scale of colours that reflects the various levels of reading difficulty. The bands are assigned by taking into account the content, the language style, the layout and phonics. Word, phrase and sentence level work is also taken into consideration.

Maverick Early Readers are a bright, attractive range of books covering the pink to white bands. All of these books have been book banded for guided reading to the industry standard and edited by a leading educational consultant.

To view the whole Maverick Readers scheme, visit our website at www.maverickearlyreaders.com

Or scan the QR code above to view our scheme instantly!

Quiz Answers: 1a, 2c, 3b, 4a, 5c